CW0086490?

Written by Kayla Willis
Illustrations by Daley Bullock
© 2022 All rights reserved.
Published by Wild Lark Books

Wild Lark Books
513 Broadway Street
Lubbock, Texas 79401
wildlarkbooks.com

#supportartreadbooks

To request permission, please use the following contact information:
Wild Lark Books - info@wildlarkbooks.com

Children's Fiction | Picture Book | Hardcover
ISBN 9781957864464
Bulk orders can be made directly through the publisher.

WILD LARK BOOKS
BOOKSHOP & PUBLISHER

A Note From the Publisher

Wild Lark Books is an independent publisher that supports authors as artists.
As with all works of art, reviews help build readerships and increase the impact of the artwork.

If Kayla's story and Daley's illustrations have inspired you or your family, please help support these artists by leaving reviews online, sharing about it on social media using the hashtag of the title (#thistlethetumbleweed), or speaking about it to all of your friends.

Your support would mean the world to us.

Thank you!

Wild Lark Books
Support Art. Read Books.

Learn More About the Author at WILDLARKBOOKS.COM

From the Author:

Dedicated to Elliott Rose, for whom this book was written.

From the Illustrator:

To my mom, Denise, and her inspiring career in education. Thank you for supporting me and all of your students over the years.

THISTLE

THE TUMBLEWEED THAT COULDN'T ROLL

WRITTEN BY KAYLA WILLIS
ILLUSTRATED BY DALEY BULLOCK

On a windy day in West Texas, before daybreak
Mama and Papa Tumbleweed shook Thistle awake.

"Come on, little one, it's time for a trip!
Put your boots on. It's time to tumble and flip!"

Thistle was excited. She'd never tumbled before.
She put on her cowgirl boots, ready to explore.

Outside her family gathered: Mama, Papa, Nana, and Grandpa too.
They jumped into the wind and off they flew!

As they went, they sang:

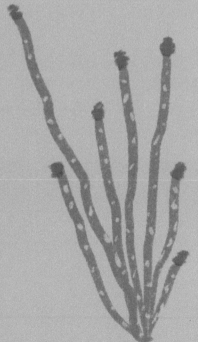

♫ TUMBLE,
TUMBLE,
TUMBLE
THAT'S WHAT WE'RE
MADE TO DO!
TUMBLE, TUMBLE, TUMBLE
I'M ON MY ♪
WAY TO
YOU!

♪

Thistle jumped for joy straight into the wind ready to chase after her family and friends.

But though the wind hit her, she didn't start whirling.
She didn't move,

she didn't budge,

she wasn't even twirling.

Even though she
tried with all her might and soul,
Thistle couldn't tumble, she couldn't even roll.

Her family was far ahead,
tumbling through the plateau,
but try as she
might, she just
couldn't go.

She tucked in
like she was taught.
She balled up, just right—or so she thought.

 Even though she was ready, she couldn't start,
and she felt a sadness deep in her West Texas heart.

Then to her right she heard a voice say, "I'm Ms. Wendy here to show you the
way. Honey, there's no time to delay, your family is getting away!"

"I know," Thistle cried, dust rolling down her face,
"I'm trying my best, but I'm stuck in place!
I can't tumble, I can't go, even though I try, I can't even roll."

Ms. Wendy understood and let out a giggle,
"Little one, you're missing what helps y'all wiggle!"

From her breeze she pulled a hat, putting it on
Thistle's head, she smiled and said, "There, that should fix that!"

And suddenly
Thistle squirmed,

she wiggled,
she shook,
she rolled,

the wind began to rumble,
and full of joy Thistle began to tumble!

She chased after her family at full speed!
So happy her tumble was finally freed.

Then she remembered she needed to thank Ms. Wendy
for helping her and, well, being rather friendly.

So, she turned, and retraced.
And found Ms. Wendy with a smile on her face.

"How did you know how to make me go?"
Ms. Wendy laughed and said
"Honey, this isn't my first rodeo!"

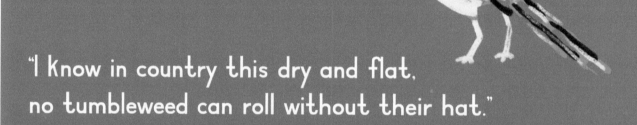

"I know in country this dry and flat,
no tumbleweed can roll without their hat."

"Now Thistle, you better get rolling or get left behind,
you should be excited there is so much to find!"

"Tumble, Tumble. Tumble
That's what we're made to do!
Tumble, Tumble, Tumble
I'm on my way to you!"

About the Author

Kayla Willis is a Texas-born author who graduated from Texas Tech University. She wrote *Thistle - The Tumbleweed That Couldn't Roll* as she drove through a West Texas Dust Storm on her way home from Lubbock, Texas to Durango, Colorado. She considers herself a "dual-citizen" of both Colorado and Texas and feels as though her time spent living in both states has allowed her to see and appreciate the beauty and uniqueness of differing landscapes, flora, and fauna. In addition to writing, Kayla is a photographer and poet. She is currently working on a publication showcasing her life through the lens. This is her first children's book.

Learn more about Kayla at wildlarkbooks.com

Enjoy a free printable coloring page featuring your favorite tumbleweed, Thistle! It is available to download at wildlarkbooks.com/thistle

About the Illustrator

Daley Bullock is an artist and illustrator from Texas, now based on the East Coast. Originally from Lubbock, Texas, her work often draws inspiration from the southwest and the desert. She graduated from Texas Tech University, where she was able to start her career in the arts and, over time, found her bright and warm artistic style. In addition to illustrating, she enjoys printmaking, photography, and renovating her Philadelphia home. This is her first children's book.

See more of Daley's artwork at daleykayestudio.com

CPSIA information can be obtained
at www.ICGtesting.com
Printed in the USA
LVHW071946101022
730379LV00008B/154